Mindanderings

Creative Classroom Approaches to Thinking, Writing and Problem Solving

by
Bob Stanish

Copyright © Good Apple, Inc., 1990

ISBN No. 0-86653-526-8

Printing No. 987654321

6050

Good Apple, Inc.
Box 299
Carthage, IL 62321-0299

Acknowledgements

Credits to:

Sharon Thompson, editor of *Challenge* magazine.

Kenneth Brousseau, photographer, for the cover photograph.

Dr. James A. Shuff, Ph.D., professor, Henderson State University
Arkadelphia, Arkansas, for the photograms and photographs.

and

for their reviews of the manuscript:

Brenda Pfaus, Special Assignment Teacher, Gifted Project,
The Carleton Board of Education, Nepean, Ontario.

Ashrita Laird and the staff of the Rainbow Mountain Children's School
Asheville, North Carolina

GA1140

Foreword

From this page "foreword," you and your students will encounter many different approaches to generating original ideas through varying thought processes. The result of these approaches to creativity—*Mindanderings*—a more effective way of thinking and writing.

Mindanderings is not a book about structure, synthesis, poetry, story writing, or thesaurus skills although it includes all of these things. It is not simply black and white although it may appear to be. It is not about concrete facts or right and wrong.

It *is* a book about choices. *Mindanderings* explores imaging, relaxation techniques, attribute listing, and patterns. It stresses the importance of the skills of observation, creativity, the free flow of ideas, and expression. Although its written word is black and white, the content vividly colors the imagination. And while abstract thinking is often condemned, here it is encouraged.

Within these pages, as in all Bob Stanish's books, he awakens the imagination by posing the powerful question "what if?" Stanish renews basic thought processes through means of rearranging, resequencing, reversing, relocating, reducing, replacing, and reordering. He relates his own imaginative ideas and unique way of looking at things to readers through the clever exercises included herein.

Mindanderings is a fine addition to the Stanish collection of creativity books. When students engage in these activities, "the processes nurtured are the behaviors bestowed. Creative thinking will expand creative potential." It is my belief that *Mindanderings* will no doubt have such an effect on you and your students.

Sharon Thompson
Editor, *Challenge* magazine

GA1140

Table of Contents

GA1140

Introduction

Strategies and Approaches

This book offers a variety of approaches toward extending creative processing and thinking into realms of original thought, written expression and problem solving. The strategy of morphological synthesis is used for quadrupling poetic production, generating inventive alternatives and for creating potential writing themes. Imagery is included for stimulating the skills of observation and written expression. Attribute listing is utilized for writing descriptive chracterizations, anecdotes and for stimulating other modes of creative written expression. Analogies and metaphorical associations are used to discover unique relationships and the skills of problem solving are nurtured through whimsical and challenging events. There are other approaches, as well. And this would include games and ideas to develop and strengthen student skills and emerging talents.

Intellectual Processes

The activities, when viewed holistically, accommodate a wide spectrum of intellectual processes known to accommodate creative effort and production. These processes would include flexibility, fluency, elaboration, originality, transformations, visualization, analysis, synthesis and evaluation.

GA1140

The Importance of Student Choice

To mind play with ideas is important. It is with this interplay that better ideas are found, where refinements are made and unique responses and solutions emerge. A number of provided structures, designs, formats and lists have been provided to encourage students to consider a variety of choices on a given problem or task. Effective ideas usually come from a multitude of ideas. Most commercial materials for classroom use do not deal with choice on a given understanding— a given concept. It is the intent of this publication to extol the virtue of choice among students in developing a product or completing a project.

The Importance of Acceptance

Several of the activities, especially the analogy-based strategies, require intellectual risk-taking. It is important early in the school year to establish a classroom climate where ideas are ventured and welcomed without ridicule. Destroyed confidence will place constraints on the confidence to produce ideas. It is worth the effort to discuss this with students. One suggestion would be to generate slogans or statements for student-created, illustrated wall posters. Visual reminders will frequently help in sustaining the effort. Support, acceptance, respect and kindness are crucial elements towards building a creative climate. Creative production is highly contingent on a creative climate.

Integrating Strategies Within Existing Curricula

The majority of strategies and much content of this book can be easily integrated within existing curricula. Morphological synthesis can be adapted to many highly structured poetic forms. The attribute lists of personality, physical and object traits will have a variety of uses towards improving word choice in writing throughout the school year. The analogy format is ideal for stimulating and improving the skills of analysis. The simile-based analogy is an excellent instructional strategy for assessing student conceptual understandings. Webbing techniques to generate prewriting information can be used extensively in many subject areas.

GA1140

Definitions

There are a few terms that are used extensively throughout this book. For an understanding of their purposes, these definitions are provided:

> *Attributes, Attribute Lists, Attribute Listing:* Attributes are basically characteristics, dimensions or parts of something. Attribute lists contain lists of characteristics, dimensions or parts of something. Attribute listing is a technique for generating ideas. In generating the attributes of something, a certain attribute or attributes may be modified for a new or improved idea or the attribute or attributes may be transferred to something else for a new or improved idea. This technique is attributed to Robert Crawford (1954).

> *Metaphorical Thinking:* This usually refers to taking ideas from one context and using them in a different context. Much of metaphorical transfer is based on analogies because of their comparative qualities. Analogies within the broad context of metaphorical thinking may be metaphor-based, simile-based, personified-based or allusion-based. The concept of metaphorical thinking has had impact from the work of W. J. J. Gordon (1961) and The Synectics Corporation.

> And this our life, exempt from public haunt,
> Finds tongues in trees, books in the running brooks,
> Sermons in stones, and good in everything.
>
> Shakespeare
> *As You Like It,* Act II, Scene 1

GA1140

Morphological Synthesis: Morphology is the study of word formations. The synthesis or fusion of selected words or combinations of words into a new context of meaning is done through word columns or in some instances, a matrix. Morphological synthesis is basically an extension of the attribute listing process.

Humor and the Not So Humorous—A Balance

There is good reason for the inclusion of selected exercises that reflect the whimsical, the novel and the humorous. Humor and a "sense of humor" are basically creative and are facilitative of further creativity (Torrance, 1979). It has been reported from synectics research (Gordon, 1961) that important solutions to problems are often stimulated from humor.

It is a belief of this author that humor is an important stimulant in nurturing student originality and in promoting unique creative associations. Promoting a balance of the serious and using humor for instructional, creative and other purposes in a classroom is a judgmental and intuitive element. There is no formula—just a "knowing" one.

And Finally. . .

The processes nurtured are behaviors bestowed. Place emphasis on the processes of creative thinking and the skills of creative thinking will expand creative potential. This is a magnificent truth within the dimensions of the human intellect. All of us can deliberately be made to think more creatively.

GA1140

Structuring for Synthesis

Morphological synthesis uses the interplay of concepts between columns to create ideas. This page contains five-syllable, first-line phrases. The next page contains seven-syllable, second-line phrases and the succeeding page contains five-syllable, third-line phrases.

Synthesize phrases from each page to create interesting three-line haiku poetry.

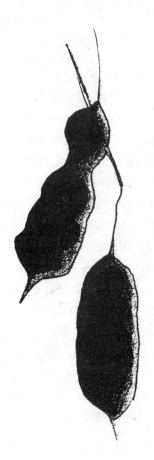

First-Line Phrases

Dancing sun shadows
Cold siren windsong
Gentle wind and rain
Melodic starlight
Strands of gossamer
A long moon shadow
Falling colored leaves
Bright chrysanthemum
Aging memories
Gentle, joyful dream
Deafening silence
Silent grounded fog
Glowing mind embers
Shining spider webs
Misty morning air
A shimmering pond

Select a phrase and write it on paper for the first haiku line.

GA1140

Structuring for Synthesis

We can, within any curriculum, create structures to see the structural components of content. In doing so, learning becomes easier, warmer and meaningful. It does this because it broadens a base of selection.

Second-Line Phrases
Interrupting mindful thoughts
Accompanies my silence
Intrude upon idle dreams
Searching silently for me
On a lonely traveled path
Reawakens my consciousness
Entering my inner self
Finding my wandering mind
Disrupting thoughts of the day
Lengthening my hurried time
Images to remember
Wanes tired lingering concerns
Like flickering candlelight
Awakens my presence here
Warming visions of the day
Musical strands of vision

Select a phrase and use it for the second line of the haiku.

GA1140

Structuring for Synthesis

In selecting lines from the three columns to create haiku, there are hundreds and hundreds of individual haiku possibilities. For sure, some will be of great beauty and some of lesser beauty. But the important thing is we have multiple choices in most anything we do. It is so important to emphasize the processes for generating choices with students. Effective decisions are truly made when choices are available.

Third-Line Phrases
Warming days await
Promises delayed
On this dreary day
Fading forest light
On a peaceful day
Obligations wait
This October day
Winter's sky awaits
On this woodland path
With softening tones
A soft serenade
On this meadowland
A peaceful mindsong
On this journey home
On this closing day
For tomorrow waits

Select a phrase and use it for the third line of the haiku.

GA1140

Example:

From the first-line column:	**Strands of gossamer**
From the second-line column:	**Intrude upon idle dreams**
From the third-line column:	**On this journey home.**

Some Variations of Use. . .
Individual selection for a favorite haiku.

Place numbers (1-16) before each phrase in each column and randomly select on the basis of sequence, for example, 2-16-3.

Challenge students to create a first line or a second line or a third line of haiku. Use the line to accommodate two provided lines from the remaining columns.

Challenge students to write two original haikus using the morphological synthesis technique. In doing this, various combinations can be made to create eight haikus. Then have them select their favorite from the eight.

Haiku has, of course, a 5-7-5 syllabic structure. Tanka is a five-line poem with 5-7-5-7-7 syllabic structure. Use the three columns to create five-line tankas. In doing this, three choices will be needed from the second-line column. Use some of the preceding variations with the tanka form.

GA1140

Morphological Synthesizing for Story Writing Themes

Tell about some possible story themes you could write about by selecting three random choices from the three columns in the matrix.

Example: 4-2-1 This is a story about *Barbara*, who wanted *acceptance from her classmates*, but her *shyness* was a problem she had to overcome.

Characters	Purpose	Obstacle
1. Joe	1. role in a school play	1. shyness
2. Cindy	2. acceptance from classmates	2. untrue gossip
3. Bill	3. friends	3. jealousy
4. Barbara	4. part-time work	4. overly protective parent
5. Bob	5. being a member of a team	5. physical handicap
6. Jane	6. organizing a club	6. home responsibilities

Now select one possible theme and think of a way to overcome the obstacle for a written story.

GA1140

Morphological Synthesizing for Story Writing Themes

This exercise is similar to the strategy developed by Fran Stryker who wrote "The Lone Ranger" radio scripts for daily weekday broadcasts. Stryker's process has been advocated by Doris Shallcross (Shallcross, 1981) for classroom creative writing purposes. Shallcross's morphological structure consists of four columns: character, goal, obstacle and result.

Suggestions

Encourage students to expand the columns with choices of their own for more story themes.

Encourage students to brainstorm possible obstacle solutions for the obstacle selected, then select one having the most appeal.

Discuss how it would be possible to write daily television soap opera themes using this approach.

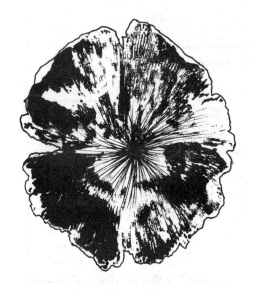

By viewing varying combinations of existing ideas, new ideas are manufactured in astonishing numbers.

GA1140

Morphological Synthesis and Invention

Inventive ideas can be generated from a morphological strategy. Use ideas taken from the "Ideas for Improvement" column to improve something.

Try something like an automobile panel or a grocery shopping cart or a refrigerator or something of your own choosing for improvement. Then select three or four ideas for improving it.

Item for Improvement

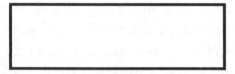

Describe in writing how the item was improved.

Ideas for Improvement

hinges
word memory calculator
digital calculator
Velcro strip
price scanner
magnets
clips
inflatable containers
disposable containers
cassette recorder
replaceable sponges
timer
extension arms
foam rubber
handles
magnifying glass
interchangeable colors
computer and accesso-
    ries, including a "mouse"

GA1140

Ask for written descriptions and drawn sketches.

Provide opportunities for students to share their ideas with classmates.

Encourage discussion on how items are improved by integrating attributes derived from other things, that is, adding a thermos concept to drinking cups, adding Velcro to clothes, adding a key case to running shoes, adding different flavors to existing food flavors, etc.

Have students, in teams, create a column of improvement ideas like those on the preceding page. Use selected ideas to improve the function of classroom bulletin board combinations.

Inventiveness is but a kaleidoscope of ever changing patterns— a portion from one pattern is added to the portion of another pattern for an improved prospectus of being. Inventiveness is not limited to machines and physical entities, for it can be reflected in words, paint, food, dance, sound, design, construction, problem solving and the acts of transforming existing concepts into different realms of viewing and being.

It is important to provide for and nurture inventiveness in children, for it widens their potential for future achievement.

GA1140

The Whimsical

Write a whimsical paragraph using all phrases listed below. Add only verbs, articles and prepositions.

sniffy sniffles
Sarah Sandpiper
scrambling seagulls
spicy spaghetti sauce

stereophonic sound
Steven Steeplechase
shopping store
silly somersaults

slender skateboards
stormy skies
slippery sidewalks
smirking strangers

_____

_____

_____

_____

_____

_____

_____

_____

_____

GA1140

Using the Whimsical for the Teachable Moment...

Alliteration is the occurrence in a phrase of two or more words having the same initial sound. The exercise phrases are alliteration examples—although somewhat ridiculous. Students will enjoy sharing their creations. Give them opportunities to do so.

- Create beautiful sounding phrases of alliteration. Use repetition of one word to generate extensions, for example:

    silhouetted streams of *starlight*
    starlight serenade
    starlight shadows

- Recall song lyrics that contain alliteration.

- List names and products that contain alliteration.

- Look for examples of alliteration in both prose and poetry.

- Think of commercial television ads that use alliteration.

- Think of alliteration as having functions. How many different functions might it serve? (repetition of sound, as a mnemonic device for remembering, as a lyrical component to accompany musical sound, to create humor in written composition, as a poetic tool, etc.)

- Think of alliteration as not having words but of having sounds. What musical compositions and songs would have alliteration of repeating notes?

- Think of alliteration as having texture. What textures would have alliteration of repeating patterns?

GA1140

Cinquainographies

Cinquain is a poem of five lines. We will alter slightly some of the requirements of a cinquain to accommodate a cinquainography. A cinquainography is a cinquain about an actual person or a fictional character.

first line.	The first name of the person.
second line.	Two words associated with the person.
third line.	Three participles or *ing* words describing one aspect of the person or character.
fourth line. . . .	Four participles or *ing* words describing a different aspect of the person or character.
fifth line.	The last name of the person.

-Example-

Abraham
American President
Rail-splitting, wrestling, reading,
Law-making, debating, presiding, emancipating
Lincoln

_____
Your first name

_____
Two words you can associate with yourself

_____
Three *ing* words describing one aspect of your life

_____
Four *ing* words describing a different aspect of your life

_____
Your last name

                                    GA1140

Cinquainographies and Some Varied Uses . . .

Write cinquainographies. . .
- on the featured person of a biographical or autobiographical story.
- on an antagonist and on a protagonist within a story.
- on a famous inventor or musician or artist.
- on a historical name.
- on your future self.
- on a favorite person or someone you admire.

Cinquainographies may provoke an interesting analysis and converging synthesis of a personality's life. Use it as stimulator for classroom discussions on personalities and biographical information studied.

One of the values in doing this exercise on historical names is the analysis it will provoke. From the collection of events in a lifetime, what events are worthy for inclusion within a few lines of poetic structure?

GA1140

Thesaurus Rex: a Game

This game requires a thesaurus for making a transition on opposite meaning concepts.

See the example on the next page.

Directions:

- Begin by writing opposite meaning word concepts within the upper and lower boxes. In the example, the concepts are *love* and *hate*.

- Use a thesaurus to make a smooth synonym-antonym transition. In the example, the transition is from love to hate (left side) and from hate to love (right side).

- The actual transfer of meaning must be made without altering a root word. Hence, a prefix or suffix may make the transition. In the example, *favor—disfavor* and *dislike—like* serve this purpose.

- Again, make the smoothest transition possible with word choices.

A Few Suggestions:

- war and peace
- passive and aggressive
- tall and short
- bold and shy
- leader and follower
- cold and heat
- reality and fantasy
- growing and decaying

GA1140

Thesaurus Rex: a Game

Example:

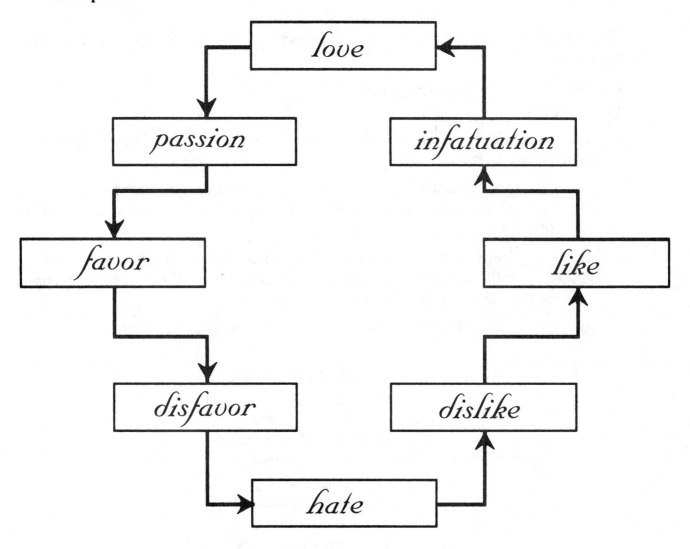

The pattern and tone of seemingly synonymous words range greatly in meaning. This exercise is meant to provide an opportunity for students to understand this. In the example, synonyms such as *love, infatuation* and *like* are many degrees apart. Challenge students, with this game, to place synonym words in the squares in both ascending and descending degree levels. To make an antonym transition requires a prefix or a suffix. Study the example on this page.

Copyright © 1990, Good Apple, Inc.

14

GA1140

Thesaurus Rex: a Game

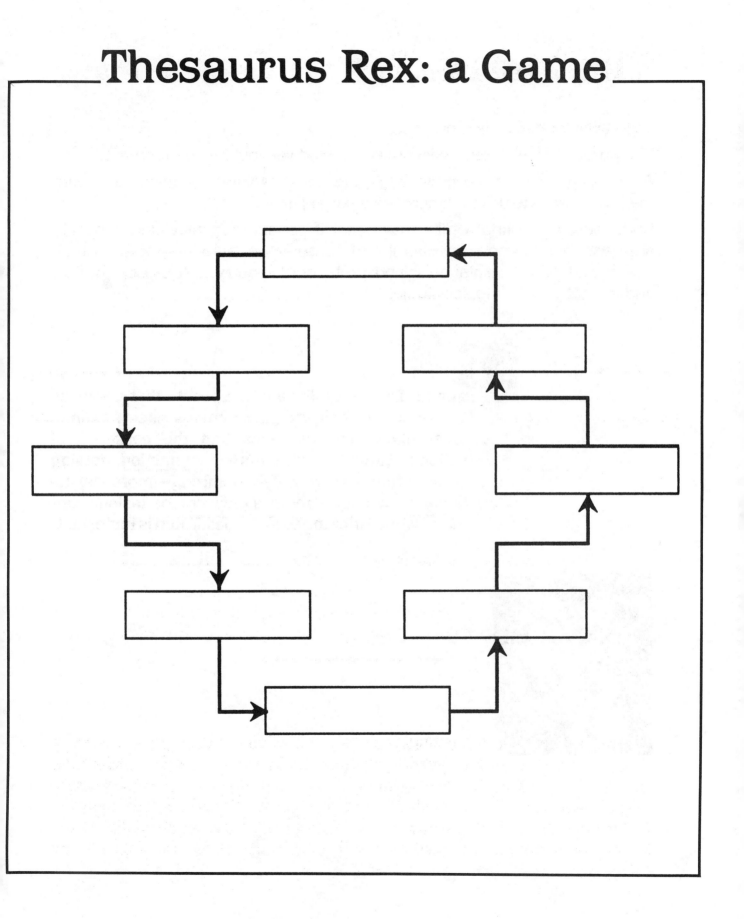

Thesaurus Rex: a Game

Page 15 is for duplication purposes.

The purpose of this exercise is for self-directed vocabulary development.

After using a few of the provided suggestions, challenge students to create their own opposite paired concepts for game play.

Some very interesting results may occur if certain content-related concepts are used. For example, try liberal and conservative; agrarian and industrial; wealth and poverty; antagonist and protagonist; poetry and prose; physical and metaphysical, or topics studied.

Upon reflecting on life and the events that compose it, words and their variant meanings direct, redirect or misdirect our passages and the passages of nations. Within the act of human interaction, nothing is more humanizing or dehumanizing—more inspirational or derisive—more significant or insignificant than a word. Knowing this in a classroom is important.

GA1140

Create a Dot Image

Connect the dots in any way you wish to create a realistic or an abstract image. The image must be related to some element within a story you just read. Shade in with pencil or color parts of the image, if you wish, to accent your drawn image. Explain the image in relationship to the story's element.

GA1140

Connecting Dots . . . Except for treating certain learning disabilities, exercises that call for connecting dots to form a predetermined picture have little educational value. The dot concept can be used, however, for nurturing the skills of visualization and stimulating recall.

The exercise on the preceding page offers an opportunity for using a different approach in stimulating discussion on an assigned story.

In using the exercise in this way, tell students . . .

- **To take a few minutes and silently run images in their minds of story scenes— in a sense, to make a silent movie in their minds before beginning.**

- **It is not necessary to use all the dots. Five or less dots may be added.**

Use the drawn images to stimulate story discussion.

The word *abstract* on the exercise page can be interpreted to infer a design, a pattern or an image not drawn in a realistic sense but with a symbolic meaning to the story.

The word *element* on the exercise page can be interpreted to mean almost anything—a symbolic object, a setting, an item of importance to the plot or setting, a character, something worn by a character.

e process information in many and varied ways. By alternating ways of doing in a classroom, we become nurturers of individual student talent.

GA1140

Sensorizing the Skills of Observation

The greatest gift to any child
is in the encouragement to enlarge a field of vision.
We can only achieve what we care to see.

We collect data from the obvious. Data, however, is enhanced when wider perspectives of collection are used. The exercises and suggestions provided here are intended to extend the skills of observation.

View the vase, for at the sides are the profiles of two children.

● Use an overhead projector beam and cast a shadow of two seated students on a chalkboard. Have another student draw the **negative space** in between the two facing profiles on black paper taped to the chalkboard. Cut the negative space from the black paper and mount it on white paper.

● Allow for experimentation among students. Encourage them to view how their profiles are patterned with others on various vase creations. **Then engage discussion on how negative spaces can help us in forming patterns . . . in promoting balance . . . in gaining perspectives . . . in recognizing and remembering detail.**

GA1140

Sensorizing for Recall

● Touching

Touch raised relief features on globes and flat relief maps. View names carefully with mind and eye. Then with a blindfold on, find and name the areas recalled.

Touch rounded pebbles within a sack. Select one that has a special appeal and study it with eye and mind. Return the pebble to the sack and find it again.

● Seeing

Illustrate a plant by drawing the negative spaces between leaves first. Then complete the drawing with positive space.

Take a shelled peanut from a sack of peanuts and draw it. But do not look at the paper while drawing. It matters not if the drawn lines are fragmented. Just caress the peanut with mind and eye to capture the essence it has and draw the essence as you perceive it to be. Return the peanut to the sack of peanuts and then find it.

Arrange different geometric patterns on an overhead projector. View and study their placement through negative space. Then take from the projector the patterns and find their original placement again. Use a variety of forms studied, for example, a parallelogram, an octagon, an equilateral triangle, etc.

o really observe is to caress with mind and eye.

Playing with Images for Written Expression

There are various ways of stimulating written expression. There are various ways of stimulating written expression in which both hemispheres of the human brain are involved, and this is one of those ways.

In preparing for this exercise. . .

- Consider using removable clear tape to secure duplicated pages. The two pages should be secured in the same fashion as you see the design on the next two pages. Roll the pages yourself before administering the exercise. This will give you an idea as to the multitude of visual images possible. Students will select an image through this process and write a descriptive paragraph stimulated by that form or image.

- The eight words in the box are meant to be challenging and descriptive and for the purpose of vocabulary enhancement, as well. If you are teaching younger children, replace the words with words of your own choosing. Do not provide words that are normally found consistently in your students' written or spoken vocabularies. Select them on a basis for vocabulary development.

21

Playing with Images for Written Expression

Take a few seconds and relax. Allow your mind to be rid of concerns and the sounds around you.

When you are ready, **slowly roll these two pages together.** Do this slowly several times. Hold the two pages horizontally, as well as vertically, and do this. Try rolling the pages upside down, as well.

Allow your mind to focus on an image or a form. Repeat the procedure until the form appears again and again.

Write a paragraph describing the form, and within the written description include three words from the list of eight words on the next page. Determine the meanings of the eight words so that you can select three that would fit the description of what you saw.

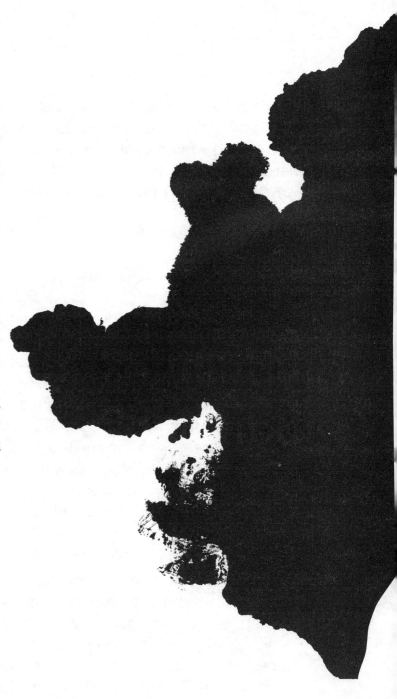

GA1140

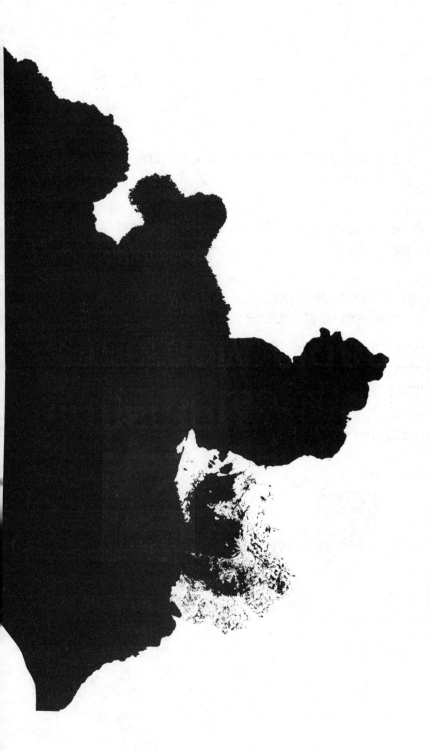

labyrinth ●

lithographic ●

reverie ●

synthesis ●

analogous ●

proliferated ●

abounding ●

exoteric ●

23

GA1140

Variations:

- By rolling the design. . .

    Determine images that can be associated with certain elements of a story previously read. Explain the elements.

    Determine images that can be associated with natural life-forms . . . with futuristic forms. Explain the associations.

- Create new designs with color tempera and paper. Fold the paper for rolling purposes. Use the designs discovered to stimulate written expression.

- As a class, list as many different forms an image may suggest. Use the image in this exercise for this purpose.

- Discuss the importance of imaging or images to the processes of thinking and writing.

We can create structures to see the structure of anything.

GA1140

Characterization Through Attributing

Try combining the intellectual processes of analysis and synthesis with the instructional strategy of attribute listing for the improvement of written expression.

On the two following pages are two listings. One list consists of **Personality Attributes.** The other list consists of **Physical Attributes.** Provide copies of both listings to students.

Guidelines:

Select a few attributes from both lists to write character sketches. Character sketches may consist of a sentence or several sentences.

Options:

1. Write character sketches on main characters from a story.
2. Write character sketches on historical names.
3. Write character sketches on favorite story characters.
4. Write character sketches on favorite comic strip characters.
5. Write a character sketch on a biographical subject.
6. Write character sketches on favorite well-known personalities.
7. Write a character sketch on yourself.
8. Write a character sketch on your future self.
9. Write character sketches on contemporary world leaders.
10. Write character sketches on friends or pets.

Example of a character sketch (selected attributes are in italics):

Albert Einstein was both *absent-minded* and an *analytical* genius who revolutionized the field of physics. *Short* of stature with *unkempt* hair, his *pleasant*, *soft-spoken* and *quiet* manner reflected his *gentle* and *humble* nature.

GA1140

Personality Attributes

absent-minded	forgetful	persuasive
active	forthright	pessimistic
affectionate	frightened	philosophical
aggressive	genius	pleasant
aloof	gentle	precise
ambitious	gleeful	prudent
analytical	grief-stricken	pushy
angry	guilty	quiet
argumentative	happy	radical
artistic	hateful	realistic
astute	honest	reflective
assertive	humble	relaxed
boisterous	hysterical	remorseful
bragging	ill-tempered	reserved
brash	imaginative	sad
brave	immature	sarcastic
bubbly	impish	sense of humor
bullying	impulsive	serene
caring	intelligent	shrewd
clever	introverted	shy
clinging	jealous	smart
clowning	kind	somber
comical	liberal	sophisticated
confident	logical	stupid
conscientious	lonely	suspicious
courteous	loud	talented
cowardly	mature	tearful
creative	mad	tender
cynical	mischievous	tense
discourteous	moralistic	tough-minded
defensive	nervous	thoughtful
dependable	neurotic	timid
depressed	no-nonsense	threatening
dishonest	obnoxious	troubled
dreamer	obsessed	uncontrolled
erratic	opinionated	undisciplined
ethical	optimistic	upset
excitable	outgoing	urgent
expedient	outlandish	venturesome
extravagant	passive	visionary
extroverted	patriotic	weak
flexible	practical	wise

GA1140

Physical Attributes

aged	gray hair	rawboned
angelic face	graying	receding hair
auburn hair	green eyes	red faced
average build	grinning	red hair
awkward	hairy	robust
bald	handsome	rough looking
baldish	hazel eyes	round-shouldered
beautiful	healthy	scars
bearded	heavy	scrawny
black hair	heavy-set	short
blue eyes	high cheekbones	short hair
blond	impish grin	sickly
boyish looking	lanky	sideburns
brunette	large	slender
braids	lean	slick haired
brown eyes	lengthy	smiling
bushy eyebrows	light skin	smirking
chunky	lopsided grin	soft-spoken
chiseled features	menacing smile	square-shouldered
clean	messy	squinty-eyed
cleanly shaven	middle aged	staring
curly hair	muscled	stocky
dainty	muscle-bound	stooped
dark eyes	mustache	straight hair
dark hair	narrow waisted	stunning
dark skin	nattily dressed	sunburned
delicate	neatly dressed	tall
dimples	neatly groomed	tanned
dirty	olive skin	thin
distinguised	overweight	trim
flaring nostrils	petite	ugly
fragile	pimples	unattrative
freckled	piercing eyes	underweight
friendly smile	pockmarked	unkempt
frowning	poker face	well-dressed
gangly	ponytail	well-groomed
glamorous	potbellied	whiskers
gorgeous	pretty	wiry
graceful	protruding eyes	wrinkled
gray eyes	rangy	youthful

GA1140

Characterization Through Attributing

An attribute is a characteristic. All forms, living and nonliving, have attributes. Attribute listing on a given form is to denote the properties or characteristics it has.

Students when asked to write descriptive sentences are often expected to express themselves in eloquent and expressive ways on the subject selected or assigned. In many instances the difficulty lies with the immediate recall of appropriate words or a time factor in finding appropriate words.

Providing attribute listings within categories of meaning has several positive benefits in promoting descriptive and expressive writing.

- accessible divergent choices from which to choose
- encouragement to analyze and converge
- encouragement to synthesize and review
- direct application with high transfer potential
- vocabulary enhancement

It is strongly suggested that the two listings—**Personality Attributes** and **Physical Attributes**—are used extensively throughout the school year. The listings are not, of course, complete. Should words on the lists stimulate through association other words not listed, then the same purpose is manifested. For teacher convenience, see the **Character Sketch Format** for stories or personalities assigned.

Wars and compromises, understandings and misunderstandings, successes and failures may be based on the appropriateness or inappropriateness of a single word.

GA1140

Character Sketch Format

Character: _____

Source: (circle appropriate category or categories) fictional book, autobiography, biography, short story, reference or textbook, periodical or other. If other, specify. _____

Title of Source:_____

Attribute Words Associated with Character

_____   _____

_____   _____

_____   _____

_____   _____

Character Sketch

_____

_____

_____

_____

_____

_____

_____

_____

_____

_____

GA1140

The most important human attributes are the attributes of . . .

●aspiring
and dreaming●
believing and
doing●
choosing and
acting●
accepting and
assisting●
determining and
reflecting●
trying and
discovering●
giving and
receiving●
cooperating and
sharing●
knowing and
becoming●
initiating and
assessing●
imagining and
creating●
venturing and
assimilating●
attending and
responding●
inquiring and
seeking●
caring and
loving●

growing and
extending●
redoing and
improving●
confronting and
proclaiming●
adapting and
changing●
feeling and
empathizing●
esteeming and
valuing●
challenging and
respecting●
committing and
cherishing●and
one without an
"ing" ending:
integrity●

GA1140

Writing Make-Believe Anecdotes

Use the **Object Attributes** form on the next page to select attribute words for writing an imagined anecdote involving an object, thing or event. An anecdote is a short account of an interesting or humorous incident.

Guidelines:
Select words that would appear to fit a selected object, thing or event. Use the selected words within sentences. Combine sentences into paragraphs for a descriptive, humorous and highly imaginative rendering on the selected object, thing or event.

Objects, Things or Events for an Anecdotal Description

Select one.
1. Eating a Piece of the World's Worst Tasting Pie
2. Carpet Mites
3. Working on a Worm Farm
4. My First Encounter with a Psychologically Impaired Alien
5. The Houseplant That Wouldn't Stop Growing
6. The Bottle of Overactive Dishwashing Detergent
7. Making Mush for Industrial Uses
8. Androids at Cash Register Checkouts
9. A Box of Nondisposable Glitter
10. Maintaining a Mud Turtle Preserve
11. Soap Bubbling as an Olympic Event
12. Putting Bad Smells and Sights into Diet Foods
13. An Encounter with a Large, Genetically Produced Cockroach
14. The Salon for Pedigreed Pets

GA1140

Object Attributes

airy	geometric	perforated	spindly
angled	glistens	perfumed	spiral
angular	glitter	plastic	spiralling
bitter	gold-like	porous	spongy
blotches	golden	powder	springy
bony	grainy	powdery	square
bouncy	gummy	puffy	squared
bouncing	hair-like	putrid	squashed
branches	hairy	reflecting	squeaky
branching	hard	reflects	squishy
bumps	hot	rough	star-like
bumpy	icy	ridges	star-shaped
clean	irregular	ridged	sticky
clear	leafy	rod-like	stringy
coarse	liquid	rounded	striped
coils	limbs	salty	sugary
coil-like	liquidy	sappy	sweet
cork	loose	scent	tall
cork-like	loose-fitting	scented	tart
crunchy	magnetic	scratchy	texture
dark	magnified	shallow	textured
diluted	meaty	shell-like	thin
dots	meandering	shiny	tight
dotted	messy	silvery	tiny
dull	metallic	slender	translucent
dusty	microscopic	slimy	transparent
dry	mirrors	slippery	triangular
eliptical	mirror-like	slinky	vapors
faded	muddy	slushy	veins
feathery	mulchy	small	veiny
fibers	murky	smelly	watery
fibery	narrow	smooth	web
flimsy	nutty	soapy	web-like
fluffy	oily	soft	wide
foamy	opaque	sparkling	willowy
follicles	oval	spherical	woody

Writing Make-
Believe Anecdotes

Suggested Sequence:

- Distribute copies of the **Object Attributes** form to all students.

- Provide the listing of topics from the preceding page and have students select one topic. Use the information, also on the preceding page, to define an anecdote. Although anecdotes are generally true accounts, have students write the imagined anecdotes in a realistic but humorous way.

- Have students use a minimum of five selected words from the list of Object Attributes per each page of writing. The selection should be made before writing is begun. By selecting the words first, some thoughts will occur on the direction of the anecdotal story. For teacher convenience, a format is provided. See **Anecdote Format** on the next page.

- This exercise will provide some interesting imaginary anecdotes. An ideal follow-up would be to have students write about an actual anecdotal experience. By providing the three lists of attributes—**Personality Attributes, Physical Attributes** and **Object Attributes**—to students from this section of the book, an enhancement of descriptive written expression should occur.

GA1140

Anecdote Format

List five attribute words that will be utilized on this page for inclusion in your anecdotal story.

_____

_____   _____

_____   _____

Anecdotal Story Title:

_____

_____

_____

_____

_____

_____

_____

_____

_____

_____

_____

_____

_____

GA1140

The Overused Word Game

This game is intended to enhance vocabulary development through team cooperation and cooperative learning.

Teaching Procedures:

- Organize your class into teams of three to four members. Distribute the most advanced readers and writers evenly among teams.

- Provide each team with a copy of **The Overused Word Game: an Exercise in Cooperative Learning** on the next page. The directions for this game are on the exercise sheet along with a scoring format.

- Select a word from **A Game Beginning List** on page 37. When ready to begin, say the word, use it in a sentence and allow time for teams to generate and select four appropriate synonyms.

- Determine team point totals and announce the winning team.

After playing a few rounds, encourage group discussion on overused words and the need for finding more descriptive replacements.

Encourage students to compile a list of their three most overused words. Challenge them to look through returned writing assignments and paperwork to find these words. Combine the contributions given to you for a total class list. Play **The Overused Word Game** on these words periodically throughout the school year.

GA1140

The Overused Word Game

An Exercise in Cooperative Learning

You will be given a common and overused word. The word will also be given as an example in a sentence. Within the square of the synonym axis write the word. Within your cooperative team, brainstorm some lesser used synonym replacements. Select four that in your opinion will give your team the highest total of points. Write your four choices on the bold diagonal lines of the synonym axis.

- For each synonym: +4 points
- For each synonym no other team used: +4 points
- For each incorrectly spelled synonym: -4 points
- For a word that is not a synonym of the overused word: -4 points
- A perfect score is +32 points.

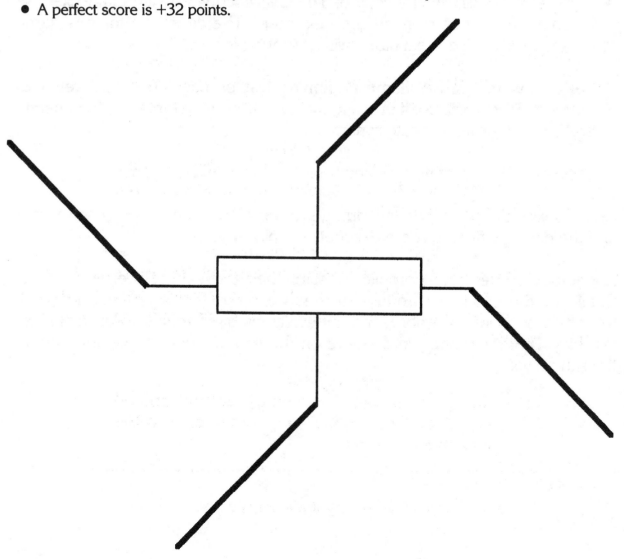

GA1140

The Overused
Word Game

The overused word is within the example sentence in bold print. Some synonym examples are below each sentence.

A Game Beginning List:

It was a **bad** day.
abominable, atrocious, awful, cursed, dreadful, heinous, horrible, horrific, miserable, poor

The game **ended.**
ceased, concluded, discontinued, terminated, consummated, expired, finished

It was **great!**
excellent, exceptional, marvelous, matchless, outstanding, splendid, stupendous, superb, tremendous, unrivaled, wonderful

She was **happy!**
blissful, cheerful, content, delighted, elated, ecstatic, enchanted, enraptured, exalted, joyful, joyous, overjoyed, rapturous, thrilled

It was an **important** discovery.
consequential, crucial, essential, eventful, foremost, key, main, momentous, notable, outstanding, paramount, pivotal, prime, prominent, significant, substantial, vital

He was **sad!**
depressed, disconsolate, distressed, doleful, grieved, joyless, melancholy, miserable, pensive, somber, sorrowful, unhappy, woeful

The above synonym list is not all-inclusive.

GA1140

All species have attributes. And some have dominant attributes. The most dominant attributes of the human species are found within the interiority of the mind.

There is differentiation among human minds and the attributes within. Some attributes of the mind have the potential for creating a greater order and some a lesser order and some have greater knowing and some have lesser knowing. And it is to the greater order and to the greater knowing that our survival lies. It is for this reason we must teach the skills of thinking.

A Summary:

The last three exercises, **Characterization Through Attributing, Writing Make-Believe Anecdotes** and **The Overused Word Game**, are intended to improve student word choice. In doing this, enhancement of vocabulary and written expression are nurtured. The exercises are structured to accommodate multiple uses with minimal teacher alteration. The common strand with all three is that of selection. Selection is always more effective when choices are available.

It is highly recommended that copies of the three attribute lists, **Personality Attributes, Physical Attributes** and **Object Attributes**, be made available at all times during writing activities in the classroom. It is also important that encouragement be given to students to use them as a reference for improving word selection.

GA1140

Relaxation

There are tensions that begin a day. There are tensions that end a day. With your students try this simple exercise at the beginning of a school day. Try the exercise again at the end of a school day.

The Exercise

- Close your eyes and take a deep breath and slowly allow air to leave your lungs (pause).

- Relax and take another breath and slowly allow air to leave your lungs again (pause).

- Relax your body so that places of tension escape (pause).

- Relax your mind so that concern and worry escape (pause).

- Relax your emotions so that calmness comes (pause).

- Now allow yourself a minute of peace (one-minute pause).

- Slowly open your eyes and allow your awareness to reenter this room.

Resume with scheduled events after a twenty-second pause.

GA1140

40

Relaxation

It is important, I think, within any society of complexity to provide opportunities for children in school and teachers in those schools to find moments of peace, of relaxation and time for the inner sanctuary of self.

The exercise is only intended for a few brief minutes of time. The pauses, unless otherwise indicated, are intended to encompass a moment of time of approximately ten to twenty seconds.

For an effective embellishment to the exercise, try music on cassette tapes. I personally have found that concertos by Vivaldo are especially stimulating.

- Try the exercise before administering a test.
- Try the exercise when things appear chaotic or argumentative.
- Try the exercise yourself before entering your classroom or when leaving school.

Much of our attention is directed towards
the exteriority of things.

So little attention is directed towards
the interiority of things,
including self.

Exteriority and interiority are not opposing forces,
but forces in need of equilibrium and balance.

GA1140

As teachers we transmit knowingly or unknowingly the frustrations of our day. Children knowingly or unknowingly transmit the frustrations of their day.

It is of greater importance today than yesterday to find moments of warmness, easiness and gentleness and time for reflection. It is important to do this within a school day. It is important for children to learn this. It is important for us to relearn this.

42

GA1140

Creative Excursions
with Writing: Episode One

Except for a window the room is darkened. I feel aloneness and hunger. Mildew is in the air I breathe, and my consciousness again returns to my captivity.

From the window I see shimmering . . .

Prewriting Preparation:
List some descriptive words that will assist you in extending the above information into a written page. Write these words in the appropriate spaces. A few examples are provided.

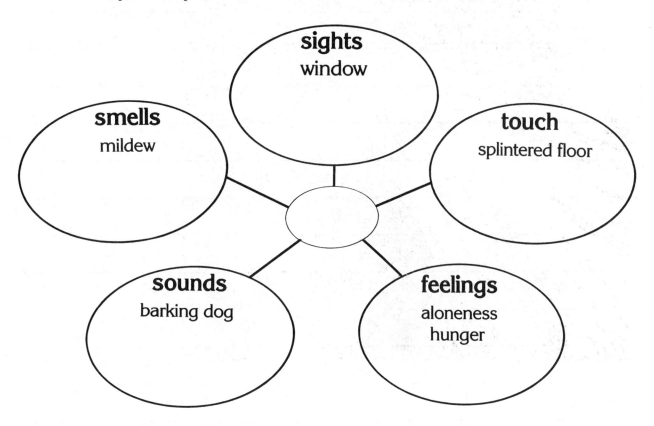

Use a thesaurus or use the list of object attributes in this book to improve your word choice.

GA1140

Episode One

Directions:
Complete this page by including some of the words listed in your pre-writing preparation.

Except for a window the room is darkened. I feel aloneness and hunger. Mildew is in the air I breathe, and my consciousness again returns to my captivity.

From the window I see shimmering _____

_____

_____

_____

_____

_____

_____

_____

_____

_____

_____

_____

_____

_____

_____

_____

44

Creative Excursions with Writing: Episode Two

Prewriting Preparation:
Look at the categorized robotic words in the diagram.

Assignment:
Write a humorous description about a short-circuited robot in a doughnut shop. Use some of the technical words in the diagram to assist you.

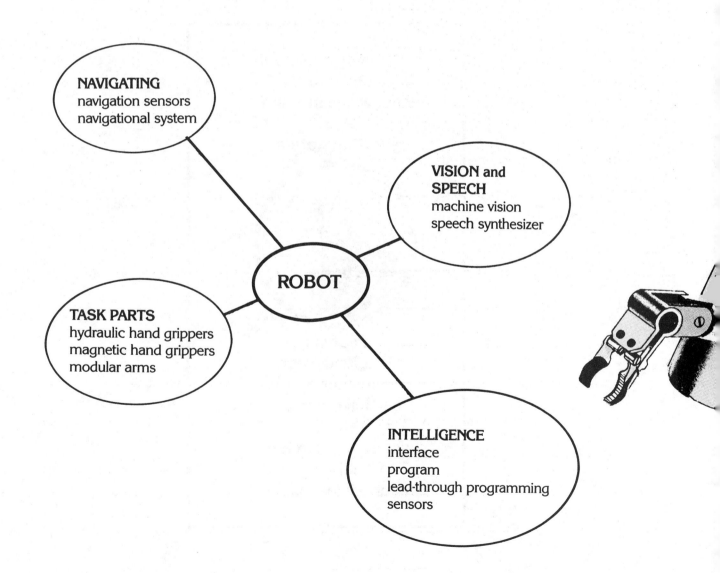

45

GA1140

Creative Excursions with Writing: Episode Three

Assignment:
Write about your first impressions of a planet as seen through the porthole of a landed spaceship.

Prewriting Preparation:
Select a minimum of six phrases and/or words from this page to enhance your sentences and written description.

wavering light rays
ecstatic
eerie, windless calm
awe
reflecting waters

skeptical
silent landscape
inspiring
earthlike forms
apprehensive
seemingly serene
foreboding
mountainless plain

GA1140

Creative Excursions with Writing: Episode Four

Prewriting Preparation:
List attributes or characteristics for each item pictured.

Assignment:
Use some of your listed attribute words in unique and exciting ways to write sentences on the following: **a tide, a spider's web** and **a piece of rock crystal.**

Example: Paper clip attribute: **bends**
   Art pad and pen attribute: **sketches**

The tide **bends** and **sketches** the shoreline edge in ever changing ways.

twists
bends

 GA1140

Creative Excursions with Writing: Episode Five

Prewriting Preparation:
On this page and the pages to follow are event scenarios that require writing. Allow the introductory remarks to caress your imaginative mind for a few written statements. Your statements may be phrases or sentences.

● On the tip of a young stem of delicate tissue, you emerge as a spike. Not a bud but soon to become one. There is the danger of killer frost and this enters your feelings. And you have thoughts of becoming a perfect leaf and free of a moth cocoon, other insects and disease. Describe your thoughts and feelings on an early spring morning of coldness and rain.

_____

_____

_____

_____

_____

● You experience strength inside of you. And you feel full and ready to burst. Describe your thoughts about becoming a bud under the warmth of a radiant sun.

_____

_____

_____

_____

_____

GA1140

● And from your budding you become a leaf. Glossy and green, your veins nourish your unblemished beauty. Describe your appearance on a perfect summer day.

_____

_____

_____

_____

● The sky brings cooling air and daylight dwindles. And your pigment of summer green is changing color. You feel dry and the outer edges of your being begin to curl. You feel less secure on the stem that holds you. Describe the colors you have and your inner thoughts and feelings on a mid-autumn day.

_____

_____

_____

_____

● You fall in a swirling, descending way. Describe the fall and your feelings on this downward journey.

_____

_____

_____

_____

_____

● Now write a complete story about life as a leaf.

GA1140

Creative Excursions with Writing: a Few Suggestions

Episode One

Encourage students to imagine themselves in the room or to imagine they were a set designer on a film project. What would be in the room? What feelings would they have being in the room? List those things that come to mind in the ovals. In writing about the room experience, words in the ovals may be accepted or rejected for inclusion.

For assistance in searching for words to place in the oval, try the attribute lists in this book or thesauruses. The description begins with the provided paragraph and the incomplete sentence in the second paragraph. Students are to make the incomplete sentence complete and then proceed with sentences of their own.

Encourage students to create a compelling description of the room's setting. And also to write a compelling description of their feelings as a captive element within that setting.

Episode Two

Before writing on this topic, engage students in a class discussion as to the kinds of things one would expect to see in a doughnut shop. Use selected words within the webbing design for technical sounding words in writing this story. Encourage students to use a satirical style of writing.

Episode Three

Encourage students to investigate meanings of the provided words and phrases. Any total of six or more provided words and/or phrases must be used within each written description.

GA1140

Creative Excursions with Writing: a Few Suggestions

Episode Four

An attribute is any characteristic an item has: For example, paper clips have attributes of **clipping** or **holding together things.** They have attributes of **bending, twisting, remolding, reshaping** and **breaking.** They also have attributes of **having thin metal** or of **plastic.** Some have the attributes of **a metallic color** and some have **many colors.** All of the preceding bold-faced words and phrases are a few of the attributes of a paper clip.

Students are to generate attributes on each of the pictured items. The items are (1) *paper clips,* (2) *an artist sketch pad with an accompanying pen* and (3) *an extending-neck desk lamp.* In the artist sketch pad and pen illustration, list attributes the two items share in association with each other, for example, shading, sketching, etching, drawing, imaging, etc., and what they independently have. Paper has flat, folding, rolling, absorbing, creasing, tearing, etc., attributes. A pen has cylindrical, marking, covercase, etc., attributes.

From attributes generated and written within the ovals, students are to select those attribute words desired to write descriptive sentences on the three topics: **a tide, a spider's web** and **a piece of rock crystal.** This exercise features the concept of attribute transfer—one of the purposes of attribute listing.

Episode Five

The prewriting preparation is for capturing thoughts and feelings of a leaf in its life cycle of three seasons. Students are to include many of these responses in their final written stories.

GA1140

52

GA1140

List Different Things That Have a Branching Pattern

Look at the photogram and see examples of branching. There are branches of government and the branching of nerve cells and rivers with their tributary branches and so many things. See how many different kinds of branching patterns you can think of and find.

_____   _____

_____   _____

_____   _____

_____   _____

_____   _____

_____   _____

_____   _____

_____   _____

_____   _____

_____   _____

_____   _____

_____   _____

GA1140

List Different Things That Have a Meandering Pattern

There are many different kinds of things that meander. Snakes move in a meandering pattern. Rivers meander and so do certain vines. See how many different meanders you can think of and find. A meandering pattern doubles back on itself before it extends out again.

_____

_____

_____   _____

_____   _____

_____   _____

_____   _____

_____   _____

_____   _____

_____   _____

_____   _____

_____   _____

_____   _____

_____   _____

_____   _____

GA1140

List Different Things That Have a Spiral Pattern

There are many different kinds of spirals. There are steeple spirals, and spirals on the shells of sea snails and spiral galaxies and so many other things. See how many different spiral patterns you can think of and find.

_____

_____

_____

_____

_____

_____

_____

_____

_____

_____

_____

_____

_____

_____

_____

_____

_____

_____

GA1140

List Different Things That Have an Explosion Pattern

There are many different kinds of things that have the pattern of an explosion. The spattering of an ink drop, certain flowers and a super nova are among this pattern. See how many different things you can think of and find that have this pattern.

GA1140

List different things that have
. . . a branching pattern
. . . a meandering pattern
. . . a spiral pattern
. . . an explosion pattern

Form cooperative learning teams with each team assigned a specific pattern.

There are many, many different things within us, on this planet and throughout the universe with these basic natural patterns. Challenge students to find as many as they can. Stimulate thinking by asking questions like . . .

What kind of a pattern is the spinal cord? . . . the nervous system?
   . . . other human systems? . . . a road system? (branching)

What kind of a pattern is a starfish? . . . a daisy?
   . . . an exploding firecracker? (explosion)

What kind of a pattern is a hurricane? . . . a rose?
   . . . the bottom of a pinecone? . . . a telephone cord? (spiral)

What kind of a pattern is a mountain road? . . . coastlines?
   . . . brain coral? (meander)

- View pictures in books and magazines and identify patterns to assist in categorizing items and things into patterns.

Metaphorical Thinking

Afterwards engage students in metaphorical thinking.

- In what ways is the human heart like a tree?
- In what ways is a galaxy like a seashell?
- In what ways is a river like thinking?
- In what ways is a wildflower like a glistening star?
- In what ways is DNA like a highway system?
- In what ways is a hurricane like a telephone cord?
- In what ways is a starfish like an explosion?
- In what ways is a shoreline like an aimless walk?

GA1140

The themes of great importance occur again and again on this planet and throughout the universe.

And it is through the thematic that instruction should be. Content has become cumbersome and it continues to expand and extend in voluminous ways.

The order of the universe can be brought into a classroom and it must be. The meandering thought embedded in haiku is not unlike the meandering attributes of a river or the meanderings of graph lines involved in technical analysis. The rhythm in good prose is not unlike the rhythm in a heartbeat or that of a symphonic composition or the rhythm of movement of particles of matter. We need to restructure content for the sake of learning and for teaching.

58

Problem Solving
with the Whimsical

There is a series of student exercises to follow. These exercises are designed to engage students, in a fun way, with the many skills of problem solving.

Exercise One (Sequencing Events)

Directions to Students:
There's a turkey buzzard roosting high in a backyard tree. The critter is making your small pet kitten highly nervous. Your challenge is to come up with a series of highly imaginative and creative events that will cause the buzzard to fly away without hurting him.

Conditions:
- In the same tree on a rope is a 100-pound weight. The rope may be cut.
- Below the 100-pound weight is a tin container with much air pressure in it. The air pressure is contained within the container by a cork.
- Add to the picture three events. The picture already contains two potential events. Event one must activate event two. Event two must activate event three. Event three must activate event four. And event four must activate event five. Event five must cause the turkey buzzard to unroost and fly away.
- Draw the events on the page and remember the events should be highly imaginative and creative. When finished, explain how your system works.

Procedures for Teachers:
- Follow procedures established in **Directions to Students** and **Conditions.**

GA1140

100 lbs.

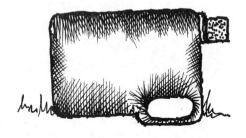

GA1140

Exercise Two (Fact-Finding)

Directions to Students:
Take the cartoon home with you and determine some facts by. . .

● looking for clues in the cartoon.

● looking at the dimensions of home closets.

● measuring distances between things.

Additional Clue:
Closet ogres do not make noises in closets. And this includes rattling wire clothes hangers with their hairy heads.

After gathering as many facts as you can, try to estimate the height and width of the largest closet ogre.

Procedures for Teachers:
● Provide copies of the cartoon, Exercise Two, to all students.

● Have them bring their findings to school.

● Look for general facts and supporting theories from students.

● Most closet doors, as the one illustrated, are about 24 inches wide. There's a window next to the door, so maybe add 6 inches and maybe 18 inches or so more due to the wall on the other side. So if the closet ogre is really stuffed into the closet, he'd have a width of something less than 48 inches. Most poles are 60 to 61 inches from the floor. Add a wire hanger to a pole and subtract 9 inches from the 60 or 61 inches for 51 or 50 inches. Since closet ogres don't rattle wire coat hangers with their hairy heads, their maximum height would be somewhat under 51 inches.

Acceptable maximum approximations for a large closet ogre are:

40-48 inches wide
44-51 inches tall
10-13 inches in depth

GA1140

Using the information you see and information you can get from actual closets, give an approximation as to the largest size possible of closet ogres. This ogre is as large as they get.

Exercise Three (Identifying Problems and Subproblems)

Directions to Students:

Read the exercise page and write what you think is the major problem within the story on paper. Also list as many subproblems as you can find and write them on paper, too! Most major problems have subproblems, and it is very important in solving the major problem to solve the accompanying subproblems. If this isn't done, we still have a problem.

Procedures for Teachers:

- Have students format their papers in this way:

Major problem: In what ways might _____?

Subproblems: 1. In what ways might _____?
                        2. In what ways might _____?
                        3. In what ways might _____?

- Have students list the major problem and subproblems on their papers.

- Arrive at a general class consensus as to what the major problem is and the accompanying subproblems.

- Brainstorm some possible solutions to the subproblems. Then decide if the major problem is solvable by solving the subproblems.

Note: Although there are varied ways of viewing the situation, the major problem would appear to be: In what ways might Mrs. Xee accommodate learning in her classroom with Slimy present? Several subproblems to this problem might consist of: In what ways might we give Slimy some positive attention so that he doesn't resort to his bizarre behavior? In what ways might we help Slimy feel better about himself? In what ways might we help Mrs. Xee solve her problem with the principal?

63

GA1140

The Situation

Another day of craziness in Mrs. Xee's classroom. She has lost control again and my head is pounding with pain. Sure would like a quiet hour in that classroom sometime.

Slimy was at it again. He's got this worm farm in his basement and I guess he gets his spending money from selling worms to fishermen. But he brings those darn things to school, sits in the classroom, and eats one or two. The class goes bananas whenever he does this. And Mrs. Xee loses control and sends Slimy to the principal. But the class is still bananas, and there's no way to quiet everyone down from that scene.

No one really pays any attention to Slimy other than his worm scene. It's the only way he seems to get attention. It's not that he's really a loner. He's only a loner because no one wants to get close to him because of the worm thing.

Now I understand that Mrs. Xee is in trouble with the principal because she can't get in much teaching with Slimy in the room. His parents don't seem to care much, and he's been paddled a lot of times. But he sure likes people to notice him and I guess, maybe, the punishment he gets is worth it to him.

GA1140

Exercise Four (Generating Solutions)

Directions to Students:
- Generate as many solutions to the problem as you can on the exercise sheet in a five-minute period of time.

- Leave your paper on your desk and circulate around the classroom looking at solutions given by other students. You have three minutes to do this.

- Return to your desk and continue writing. You might want to combine some of the ideas you saw for a new idea. Some of the ideas you saw might stimulate your mind to add some different ideas. Do this. Continue writing for a five-minute period.

- Take a few minutes and select your three best ideas and present them to your teacher.

Procedures for Teachers:
- Distribute exercise sheets and tell students to use the back side for more idea listing if additional space is needed.

- Encourage students to actually look at their own shoe tongues to help stimulate ideas while doing the exercise. Give a few examples yourself to stimulate creative thinking, for example, *use as a bookmark, a doorstop, squash termites with,* etc.

- Establish the conditions by reading the **Directions to Students** section above.

- Afterwards, discuss the importance of generating a quantity of ideas in order to gain a few outstanding ones. Ask students what factors they used in selecting their best ideas (for example, humor, practicality, originality) to give you. Indicate that in selecting ideas from a quantity of ideas that **criteria** is important. In a sense, they were using criteria to select three ideas to give to you. By viewing the ideas of others, new ideas are often stimulated and combined with existing ideas. This is known as **piggybacking** —a good way to gain additional ideas.

GA1140

How Many Different Uses for a
Detached Shoe Tongue?

_____

_____

_____

_____

_____

_____

_____

_____

_____

_____

_____

_____

_____

_____

_____

_____

GA1140

Exercise Five (Selecting a Solution)

Directions to Students:

There's a boa constrictor in a supermarket food store that has settled into a bin of Idaho potatoes. Listen carefully to the conditions of this situation; then brainstorm some possible solutions to the problem. **In what ways might we lure the boa out of the potato bin and safely capture him?**

Conditions:

- A truck transporting a 20-foot boa constrictor to a zoo stopped in the parking lot of a food store. After checking the cargo, the driver did not shut the cargo door. The snake escaped and entered the food store. It has nestled into a bin of potatoes.

- Shoppers in the food store have panicked and the manager is asking your help in solving this problem. He won't have paying customers in the store until the snake is removed. The truck driver has informed the store manager that the boa is rare due to its size and age. The zoo expects it to gain a length of 35 feet and thus draw massive crowds to the zoo to see it.

- The boa has not eaten in a month, is hungry and loves live prey. The zoo has paid several thousand dollars for the snake, and its safety is of prime importance.

- The food store is in a strip mall. Other businesses in the mall include a pet store, medical offices, a hardware store and a clothing store. The zoo is 100 miles away.

Procedures for Teachers:

- Read **Directions to Students** and the **Conditions** to your class. Provide time for solo brainstorming. Distribute copies of Exercise Five to all students and have them determine their five best ideas. Write the five ideas on the evaluation grid (items 2 through 6). Item 1 is an example. Students are then to rate their five ideas in association with the criteria and the point scale to determine their best idea of the five ideas.

In what ways might we lure the boa
out of the potato bin and safely
capture him?

ideas		safe?	affordable?	fits situation?	success likely?	minimal time?	POINTS
1	Lure him out with a mouse tied to a string; then bag him.	1	3	2	1	1	8
2							
3							
4							
5							
6							

criteria

Good idea—3 points
Average idea—2 points
Poor idea—1 point

GA1140

Exercise Six (Planning, Cooperation and Working Within the Contingencies of a Problem)

Directions to Students and Project Conditions:
- Work with a team of three or four classmates.

- As a team, select a project from a list of three project choices.

- Each team of students must provide their own materials on a day designated by your teacher.

- Each team, prior to the designated date, must plan a procedure to complete their chosen project within a time limit.

- Each team must complete their project within a time limit of forty minutes.

Procedures for Teachers:

- Provide the information cited above.

- Select a date and time for the projects.

- Distribute copies of the project descriptions.

- Assign teams.

- Encourage team planning and cooperation. Each team is responsible for the materials required. *One aspect of team planning is the determination by each team the quantities of materials required.*

Note: After the demonstration it will be evident those teams that utilized planning to meet the conditions of the selected problem. Use this as a teachable moment on the advantages of planning and cooperation in problem solving.

GA1140

Project I

Using only dried spaghetti strands and gumdrops, construct a structure that will hold 5 pounds of school books. The books must be, at a minimum, 6 inches above a floor or desk surface.

Project II

Using only small or medium-sized garbage bags, rubber bands and air from your lungs, construct a three-dimensional pyramid large enough to house three students inside. No more than 40 bags may be used. There are no limitations on the rubber bands. Bags may be bent, twisted or shaped in any fashion, but not cut or torn.

Project III

Using only Popsicle sticks, rubber bands and tape of your choice, construct a catapult that will launch a wadded piece of 8 1/2 x 11-inch paper a distance of six feet. The structure of the catapult must be taped to a desk or floor surface at the time of the launch.

On the date provided, a project must be constructed and demonstrated within a forty-minute time period.

Reordering

Rearrangement, resequencing, reversing, relocating, reducing, replacing and reordering are the r's of transforming. Transforming can cause alterations to habit-bound processes of planning and doing.

Take a chapter, a unit, an exercise, a biography studied or a story read and have students **compile answers without questions.** Then, as a class, determine questions to accommodate the answers.

Example: **The answer is Plato.**

Questions

- Who wrote *The Republic*?
- Who established the Academy, the first university of the western world, in Athens?
- Who, in addition to Socrates and Aristotle, attempted to improve government by educating young men in philosophy?
- Who tutored Dionysius?
- Who was mentored by Socrates, and who was Aristotle's mentor?
- Who wrote *The Laws*?
- In whose absence did Aristotle administer the Academy?

Note: This procedure will accommodate the sharing of information. It provides for an interesting way to extend reviews and comprehension of facts.

avor the importance of the question.
**For without it,
where would the solutions be?**

GA1140

Other Ways of Reordering...

● Reordering Cause and Effect:

Examples: 1. The effect is the greenhouse effect. Brainstorm all possible causes.

2. The effect is private enterprise. Brainstorm possible causes.

3. The effect of this story is boring. List possible causes.

● Reordering Sequence:

Examples: 1. The mathematical answer is _____. Describe or web the process that would provide the answer.

2. Read the last few pages of a story and speculate on how the story began.

3. Begin writing a narrative by writing the plot first. Then resolve the plot for an ending. And finally, write the introduction leading to the plot.

4. How many differently named polygons can be identified by reordering the placements of equilateral triangles of the same size?

● Reordering Events:

Examples: 1. What would have been the impact on modern history if the Revolutionary War was never fought?

2. Speculate on the outcomes. . .
   if the Mississippi River was only a stream.
   if the Great Wall of China was never built.
   if the atom was never split.
   if glaciers never formed.

GA1140

Metaphorical Thinking and the Simile-Based Analogy

In what ways is a river like a tree
And like ice crystals on a window pane
And like you and me
And all things in every domain?

The term *metaphorical*, in a creative sense, applies to many figures of speech. The comparative qualities of the simile, the metaphor, personification and allusion allow for agreement, similarity and resemblance. They form the basis, through imagery, of extending our perceiving, receiving, discovering, experiencing and expressing.

Analogies come in varieties of kind and use. They form a base for problem-solving processes in the corporate realm and a base for analyzing the skills of thinking in the educational realm. Used semantically by writers, symbolically by painters and satirically by comedians, they can form a potentially powerful instructional base in the classroom.

Simile-based analogies provide the true essence of metaphorical thinking. To assist in helping students make unusual and unique conceptual connections with simile-based analogies, there is a two-page graphic layout on the next two pages. Duplicate, for classroom use, these two pages and connect them with clear tape. Instructions for using the graphic will follow.

GA1140

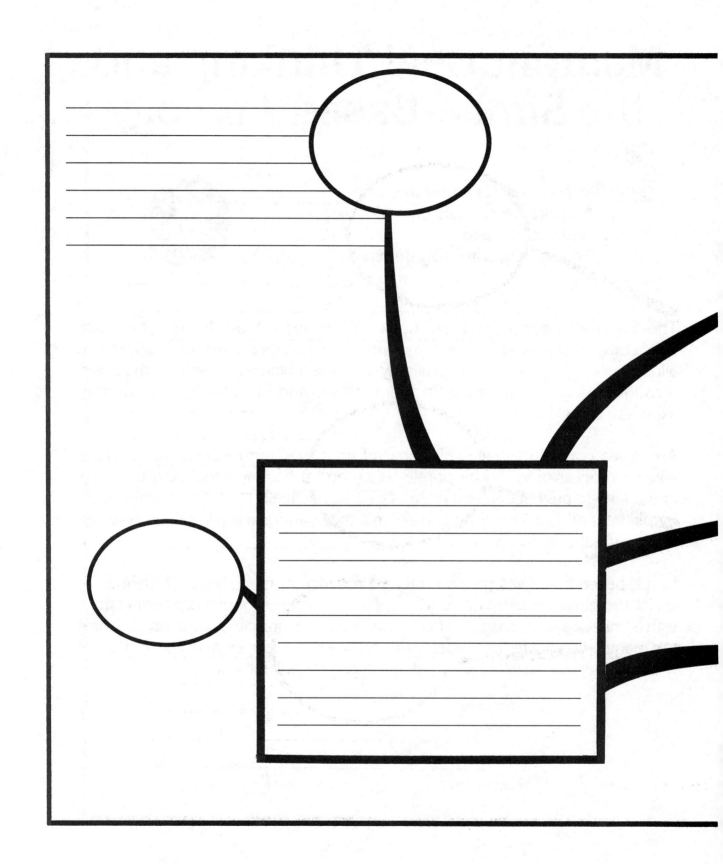

74

GA1140

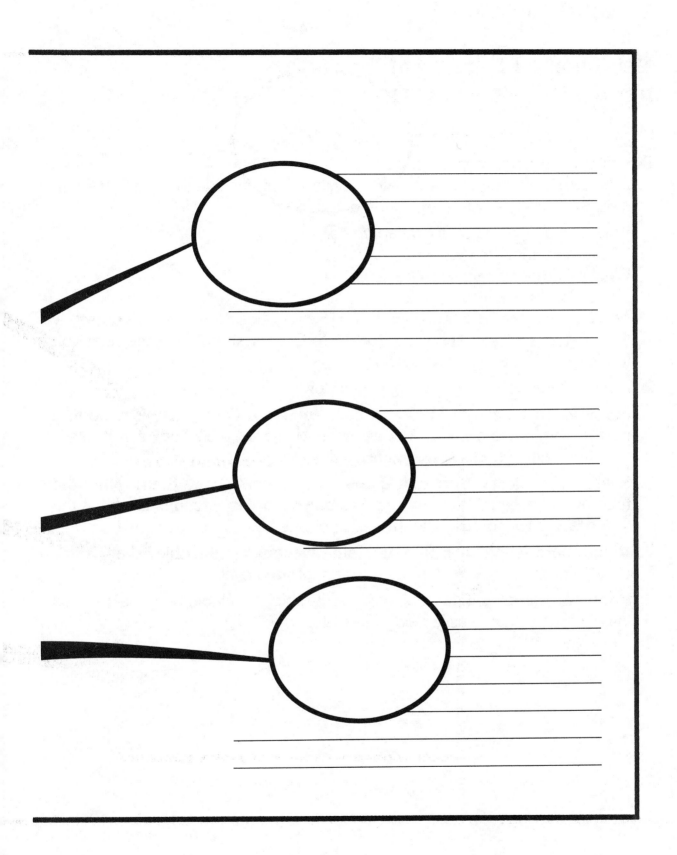

75

GA1140

Metaphorical Thinking and
the Simile-Based Analogy

Directions and Sequential Steps:

1. Determine, first of all, a concept for development. Include the *concept* within a question. Some examples might include:

    What is a *successful political candidate*?
    What is American *capitalism*?
    What determines *a literary classic*?

    The concept can be almost anything. Use a concept that you are presently teaching or one you are about to teach. Do not share the statement you formulate with students at this stage.

2. List some random concrete objects or items.

    Some examples might include a coat hanger, a desk, a shoe, a door, a mirror, a refrigerator, a microwave oven, a glossary section of a book, a telephone answering service, a paper clip, etc.

3. **Select four objects from item 2 and have students write them within the four ovals of equal size on the two-page graphic section.** Each of the four ovals will accommodate the name of one object.

4. **Do attribute listing on each of the four objects.** Write the objects' attributes on the lines that extend from the four equal-sized ovals.

    Attribute examples of a coat hanger: flexible, bendable, can be molded into various shapes, easily recognized, etc.

GA1140

Metaphorical Thinking and the Simile-Based Analogy

5. **You formulate four analogies, for comparative purposes, between the concept and the objects. Write the four analogies on the chalkboard based on the objects attributed.**

    Some objects might include:

    How is a successful political candidate like a coat hanger?
    How is a successful political candidate like a desk?
    How is a successful political candidate like a shoe?
    How is a successful political candidate like a microwave?

6. **Students are to write the concept in the smaller oval next to the box.** In our example, it would be *successful political candidate.* **Students will then select attributes previously listed they feel are related to the concept and list them within the box on the lines provided.**

7. **Use the words in the box to stimulate statements that would define or give meaning to the statement established in item 1.** For example, *what is a successful political candidate?* At this point, write the concept question on the chalkboard.

Note: Emphasize that the selected attribute words are to be used as stimulators for the statements. They may be altered in suffix, tense and form.

GA1140

Metaphorical Thinking and the Simile-Based Analogy

Examples of Statements:

- **A successful political candidate is one who may be** *easily recognized* (stimulated from the coat hanger attribute, easily recognized).

- **A successful political candidate is one who may have a** *solid* **base for** *communicating* (based on attributes solid and communicating from the object, desk).

- **A successful political candidate is one who may have a** *personal style* (shoe attribute).

- **A successful political candidate is one who may have personal** *warmth* (microwave oven attribute).

The above listing of statements may be extended by using more objects for formulating additional simile-based analogies. An easy way of doing this would be to provide different object names to different groups of students for the purpose of attribute listing. Consider teaming students in groups of two's or three's for the attribute listing segment of this strategy.

This method can provide access to some fairly complex concepts and issues. For example, try some difficult ones like *justice*, *democracy* and *international diplomacy.*

GA1140

Using Analogies to Stimulate Valuing

The answer is not important but the explanation of the answer is.

1. Which has more voltage—multiple choices or multiplying choices?

_____ has more voltage because

_____

_____

_____

_____

_____

_____

2. Which is more polluted—total agreement or agreement through compromise?

_____ is more polluted because

_____

_____

_____

_____

_____

_____

GA1140

3. Which is louder—a belief or disbelief?

_____ is louder because_____

_____

_____

_____

_____

4. Which is more durable—an entrance or an exit?

_____ is more durable because_____

_____

_____

_____

_____

5. Which is more fragile—prizing something or having something prized by others?

_____is more fragile because

_____

_____

_____

_____

Using Analogies to Stimulate Thinking

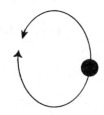

The answer is not important but the explanation of the answer is.

1. Which requires more detergent—fiction or nonfiction?

_____ requires more detergent because

_____

_____

_____

_____

2. Which requires less sleep—the periodic table of elements or a table of periodicals?

_____ would require less sleep

because_____

_____

_____

_____

_____

GA1140

3. Which has more flexibility—a right angle or a parallelogram?

A _____ has more flexibility because

_____

_____

_____

4. Which has greater intelligence—a question mark or an exclamation mark?

_____ has more intelligence because

_____

_____

_____

5. Which has greater wear—fabric or cloth?

_____ has greater wear because _____

_____

_____

_____

GA1140

Using Analogies to Stimulate Thinking and Feeling

The answer is not important but the explanation of the answer is.

1. Which has more bumps—being ignored or being criticized?

   Being _____ has more bumps because

   _____

   _____

   _____

   _____

2. Which is more tender—a word or a feeling?

   A _____ is more tender because

   _____

   _____

   _____

   _____

GA1140

3. Which contains more sensitivity—a postage stamp or a present?

A _____ has more sensitivity because

_____

_____

_____

_____

4. Which is taller—acceptance or rejection?

_____ is taller because

_____

_____

_____

_____

5. Which is more difficult to hide—success or failure?

_____ is more difficult to hide because

_____

_____

_____

_____

GA1140

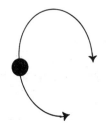

Using Analogies to Stimulate Inquiry

The answer is not important but the explanation of the answer is. Do some investigation for supporting an explanation.

1. Which is more playful—an electron or an atom?

   An _____ is more playful because _____

   _____

   _____

   _____

   _____

2. Which has the better disposition—a spiral or a meander?

   A _____ has a better disposition because

   _____

   _____

   _____

   _____

GA1140

3. Which is more tense—a graph or a chart?

A _____ is more tense because

_____

_____

_____

_____

4. Which is more playful—a metaphor or a simile?

A _____ is more playful because

_____

_____

_____

_____

5. Which is more athletic—a fiord or a strait?

A _____ is more athletic because

_____

_____

_____

_____

GA1140

Using Analogies to Stimulate Analysis of Self

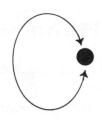

The answer is not important but the explanation of the answer is.

1. Which is easier to get along with—my thoughts or my feelings?

   My _____ are easier to get along with because

   _____

   _____

   _____

   _____

2. Which has a better time—my looks or my appearance?

   My _____ has a better time because

   _____

   _____

   _____

   _____

GA1140

3. Which is smoother—going along or getting along?

_____ is smoother for me because

_____

_____

_____

_____

4. Which is heavier to carry—a close friend or a worst enemy?

For me, a _____ is heavier to carry because

_____

_____

_____

_____

5. My mind is most like (select one)
   a. a rubber band
   b. a shoestring
   c. a paper clip

   because _____

_____

_____

_____

_____

GA1140

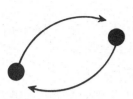

Using Analogies for Lesson Closure

One effective way of using the processes of metaphorical thinking is in closing a lesson. It is effective because unique analogy associations are called for—associations between a learned concept and a seemingly remote subject. Being able to make associations of this kind reflects understanding of the learned concept.

Here are some examples with some probable responses. Do not view the response example as being the only correct response. There are many correct answers with this type of questioning.

1. **In what ways are chemical reactions like butterflies?**

   Response example: Chemical reactions are like butterflies because change is associated with both. A chemical reaction will change a substance. Metamorphosis will change the substance of a caterpillar into the substance of a butterfly.

2. **In what ways are autobiographies like ponds?**

   Response example: Autobiographies and ponds both reflect. An autobiography reflects images of events—events that effected upon a life. A pond reflects images and events that encroach upon it.

3. **In what ways is DNA like an antique?**

   Response example: DNA is a genetic strand that is inherited. An antique may be inherited as well.

4. **In what ways is current electricity like a door?**

   Response example: Current electricity has a circuit that can be closed or opened. A door can be closed or opened. They both have attributes for being opened or being closed.

5. **In what ways are landforms like cut diamonds?**

   Response example: Landforms may be altered by natural forces. Diamonds may be altered by forces applied by man. They are both altered by forces.

GA1140

6. In what ways are electrons like mail carriers?

Response example: Electrons, if unaltered, will travel in predictable paths. Mail carriers, if unaltered, will travel in predictable paths on their delivery routes.

7. In what ways are octagons like high cholesterol foods?

Response example: Stop signs are in the shape of an octagon. Stop signs and high cholesterol foods should encourage caution and stops.

8. In what ways is gravity like perfume?

Response example: They may both attract things due to their compelling forces.

9. In what ways are effective story characters like tasty molasses?

Response example: They both have properties of appealing to our tastes—our taste for interesting character development within stories and our taste for a platter of pancakes and molasses.

10. In what ways is alliteration like a scrumptious pie?

Response example: A scrumptious pie is liable to generate repetitious sounds of alliteration among its tasters. Hmmm hmmm hmmm! Yummy yummy!

11. In what ways is a circumference like a shoe?

Response example: Both equate to size, length and measurement.

12. In what ways is an ecosystem like a Rembrandt painting?

Response example: An ecosystem is a balanced community of life-forms. A Rembrandt painting, except for still lifes, is a balanced canvas of life-forms or a life-form.

Teaching Suggestion:

In structuring questions of this type, list the concept first. Then do attribute listing on the concept. Then think of dissimilar things that share the same attribute or attributes for an analogy fit.

Item 11:

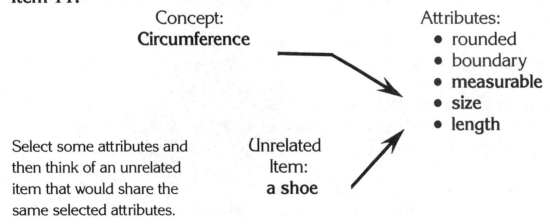

Concept:
Circumference

Attributes:
- rounded
- boundary
- **measurable**
- **size**
- **length**

Select some attributes and then think of an unrelated item that would share the same selected attributes.

Unrelated Item:
a shoe

Using Analogies. . .

- Accept all explanations.
- Look for unique associations and insight in explanations provided.

Example: Which is more tense—a graph or a chart?

A graph is more tense because some graphs, like an electrocardio-graph, can really make one nervous. Also, some graph interpretations can lead to future predictions. And maybe some of these predictions can cause tension.

or

A chart is more tense, especially if it is an eye chart or a weight chart and one is nearsighted and overweight. A navigation chart can be very tense in shark-infested waters.

Note: Some explanations given in the exercises **Using Analogies to Stimulate Analysis of Self** and **Using Analogies to Stimulate Thinking and Feeling** may warrant your analysis and assistance. Many students are seeking help but cannot find appropriate avenues to express that need. These two exercises may provide the avenue for some.

GA1140

Analogies
provoke thought into
wondrous realms of discovery
and understanding. Image
the flow of an ocean
current and comprehend
the flow of human adrenalin.
Imagine the husk of a
weed pod and view
the trajectories
of the explosion.

The
metaphorical energy
of the analogy
generates inventiveness
of thought into
unifying elements
of creative expression.

To teach
the skills of thinking
without
the analogy is like
removing buds
from a
flowering tree.

GA1140

Quick Liners

Quick Liners have appeared in several publications (Stanish, 1977, 1988 a, b, c). A few of them are repeated here plus several other new ones. Their purpose is to engage students in provocative and humorous thought. Use them in those remaining seconds between classes, waiting lines and those "let's get ready for the bell" times. Cut along the solid lines and place the Quick Liners in a shoe box or a similar container and encourage students, through random selection, to respond to the ones selected.

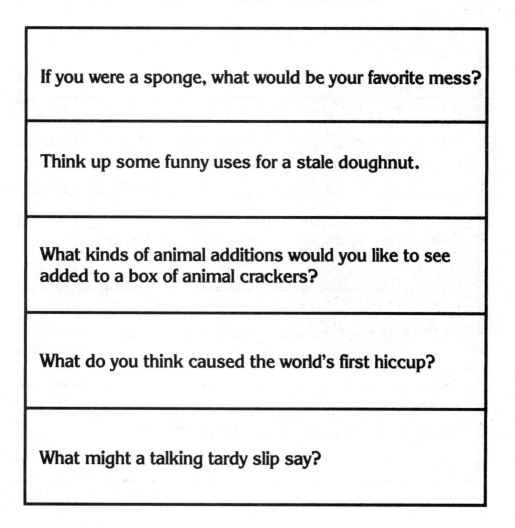

If you were a sponge, what would be your favorite mess?

Think up some funny uses for a stale doughnut.

What kinds of animal additions would you like to see added to a box of animal crackers?

What do you think caused the world's first hiccup?

What might a talking tardy slip say?

What three functions would you give to an android teacher's helper?

Think of something you'd like to give to a de-memorizer machine.

What kind of gloves would appeal to the hands of a grandfather clock? Think in terms of fabric, color and shape.

How would you dress up a chameleon so you wouldn't lose him?

What's the worst smell in a three-day-old sack lunch?

How would you dress up a real ogre on Halloween?

Think up a use for a worn pencil eraser nub.

What's the best time for a good daydream?

Plan a dinner menu for a foe.

Who "shhh's" the most among teachers?

What color would you give embarrassment if everybody was green?

Think of some lousy vegetable flavors to give to ice cream.

Where's the best place to hide a Twinkie if you're seated in the principal's office?

Give a new function for a smudge of peanut butter.

How would you explain to an octopus the best way to put on a pullover octopus sweater?

What's the best thing to crunch and chew to gain someone's attention?

GA1140

Where would you relocate a bothersome freckle?

What's the best way to get an adult out of a room?

What would you wear in bad taste to a bad taste party?

Think up five uses for Cinderella's glass slipper.

If all olives replaced cherries and all cherries replaced olives, what servings of what would be the most difficult to eat?

If you were a human clock, at what times would you prefer your arms?

What numbers on your telephone hurt the most?

Define an "icky."

GA1140

Think up some unusual uses for chewed chewing gum.

Try pronouncing your full name without syllables.

Describe what a tooth fairy looks like.

Think of a word that has a funny sound when spelled backwards.

Make the funniest face you can make.

Where wouldn't you take a time machine?

Think of something you wouldn't mind losing.

Where would you go on a magic carpet?

GA1140

What kind of a situation would be a good situation to become invisible?

What kind of a new eating utensil would you design for eating peas?

Do your best blank stare.

What kind of a bumper sticker would you create to stop people from reading bumper stickers?

What would cause your teacher to have a day nightmare?

Suppose you could take a UFO on a guided tour. Where would you take it?

How would you draw the word *tickle* to define its meaning?

If silence was in a spray can, what would you spray?

GA1140

Create a word for accidental clumsiness.

What's the best way to squeeze a sneeze?

Which letter swims better in alphabet soup?

What would go into the design of a cookie jar to scare away cookie monsters?

Think up an original excuse for not doing a homework assignment.

What Dr. Seuss character would make an interesting substitute teacher?

How would you write umpteenth as a numeral?

What edibles do you think are in your teacher's middle desk drawer?

GA1140

What makes the worst mess on a T-shirt—a squiggle or a splot?

What's the best way to fake out a teacher into thinking you know an answer you don't know?

What would make for the worst squishy in a back pocket?

What would you do with a unicorn?

Quick Liners

- Accept all answers and encourage supporting explanations.
- Look for unique, unusual and clever responses.
- Afterwards ask: Was there a question that someone else had that you wished you had? What was it and what's your answer?

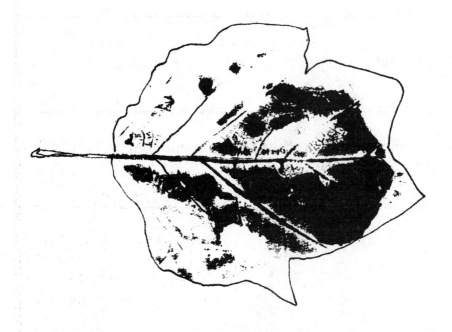

GA1140

References

Crawford, Robert P. *The Techniques of Creative Thinking.* Englewood Cliffs, New Jersey: Prentice-Hall, 1954.

Gordon, W. J. J. *Synectics.* New York: Harper & Row, 1961.

Shallcross, Doris J. *Teaching Creative Behavior.* Englewood Cliffs, New Jersey: Prentice-Hall, Inc., 1981.

Stanish, Bob. *Sunflowering: Thinking, Feeling, Doing Activities for Creative Expression.* Carthage, Illinois: Good Apple, Inc., 1977.

_____ (a) "Quick Liners for a Sunny Day." *Challenge*, 1988, 7(1), 31.

_____ (b) "Quick Liners for a Rainy Day." *Challenge*, 1988, 7(2), 32.

_____ (c) "Quick Liners for a Cloudy Day." *Challenge*, 1988, 7(3), 33.

Torrance, E. Paul. *The Search for Satori and Creativity.* Buffalo, New York: The Creative Education Foundation, 1979.

A Few Highly Recommended Readings on Creativity

For a comprehensive, research-based and historical understanding of creativity:

Isaksen, Scott G., ed. *Frontiers of Creativity Research: Beyond the Basics.* Buffalo, New York: Bearly Limited, 1987.

For a comprehensive understanding of creative problem solving:

Isaksen, Scott G., and Donald J. Treffinger. *Creative Problem Solving: The Basic Course.* Buffalo, New York: Bearly Limited, 1985.

For an excellent overview of techniques and strategies appropriate for classroom use:

Davis, Gary A. *Creativity Is Forever,* 2nd Edition, Dubuque, Iowa: Kendall/ Hunt Publishing Company, 1986.

From the master—an excellent resource for nurturing creativity in one's self and others:

Torrance, E. Paul. *The Search for Satori and Creativity.* Buffalo, New York: The Creative Education Foundation, 1979.

GA1140

An Epilogue

Within
many branching structures
like with trees
there is both root and canopy.
It is difficult for a root to see the canopy.
And it is difficult for a canopy to see the root.
They can only envision the other.

A canopy cannot be much of a canopy without a root.
A root cannot be much of a root without a canopy.
They both require the other.

Within
many branching structures
like with schools
there is both root and canopy.
It is difficult for a root to see the canopy.
It is difficult for a canopy to see the root.
They usually only envision the other.

A canopy cannot be much of a canopy without a root.
A root cannot be much of a root without a canopy.
They both require the other.

I would like to see teaching practitioners
in the canopies of legislative decision-making,
if just for a moment in time.

I would like to see legislative decision-makers
in the roots of the practitioning system,
if just for a moment in time.

In doing this, envision could become vision.
We both require the other.

GA1140

103

GA1140

Notes

The **white images on black** are photograms. Photograms are pictures created without a camera. They are created by placing objects between the light beam of an enlarger and a sheet of light-sensitive paper. The paper, after exposure, is processed in the normal way. The photograms were done by Dr. James Shuff.

The **black images on white** are a combined synthesis of illustration with a simple ink print. These, along with the illustrations, were created by Bob Stanish.

The type of activity **analogies** on pages 73 through 91 are direct and personal analogies as defined by the synectics corporation. A direct analogy requires a comparison between unrelated concepts. A personal analogy requires an identification of self with an object, process or factor.